# When Will Sarah Come?

Story by **Elizabeth Fitzgerald Howard**

Pictures by **Nina Crews**

 Greenwillow Books, New York

**For Jonathan and Sarah
and Granddaddy,
with love**
**–E. F. H.**

**For Grandma**
**–N. C.**

The art was prepared from full-color photographs. The text
type is Akzidenz Grotesk Black. Text copyright © 1999 by
Elizabeth Fitzgerald Howard. Illustrations copyright © 1999
by Nina Crews. All rights reserved. No part of this book may
be reproduced or utilized in any form or by any means,
electronic or mechanical, including photocopying, recording,
or by any information storage and retrieval system, without
permission in writing from the Publisher, Greenwillow Books,
a division of William Morrow & Company, Inc.,
1350 Avenue of the Americas, New York, NY 10019.
www.williammorrow.com
Printed in Singapore by Tien Wah Press
First Edition 10 9 8 7 6 5 4 3 2 1

Library of Congress Cataloging-in-Publication Data
Howard, Elizabeth Fitzgerald.
When will Sarah come? /
story by Elizabeth Fitzgerald Howard; pictures by Nina Crews.
    p.   cm.
Summary: A little boy waits and listens all day for his older
sister to come home from school.
ISBN 0-688-16180-4 (trade).   ISBN 0-688-16181-2 (lib. bdg.)
[1. Brothers and sisters–Fiction.
2. Afro-Americans–Fiction.]   I. Crews, Nina, ill.   II. Title.
PZ7.H83273Wj   1999   [E]–dc21   98-42169   CIP   AC

**Sarah is a big girl now.
She went to school today.**

I stay home with Grandmom.
I build with my blocks.
And wait for Sarah.

**I want to play with Sarah.
When will Sarah come?**

I ride my big, red fire truck.
**ZOOM ZOOM BARRUMMM!**
I want to ride with Sarah.

# FLIP-flap-plop.

## PLOP.

Who is that?
What is that?
Is it Sarah?

**No, it isn't Sarah.
It's Mrs. G., our mail lady,
pushing letters in the letter slot.**
*FLIP-flap-plop.* PLOP.

When will Sarah come?

**I pull my teddy bear.**
**And wait for Sarah.**

I push my
teddy bear.
And wait
for Sarah.

I ride my big, red fire truck.
**ZOOM ZOOM BARRUMMM!**
Sarah likes my fire truck.

# CLIP... CLIP...

# TRRRR.

# TRRRR.

# CR CRICK.

**Who is that?**
**What is that?**
**Is it Sarah?**

No, it isn't Sarah.
It's the tree trimmers cutting
old, dry branches off.
CLIP . . . CLIP . . . TRRRR. TRRRR. CRCRICK.
When will Sarah come?

I make
play cake
and wait
for Sarah.

I blow shiny
bubbles
and wait
for Sarah.

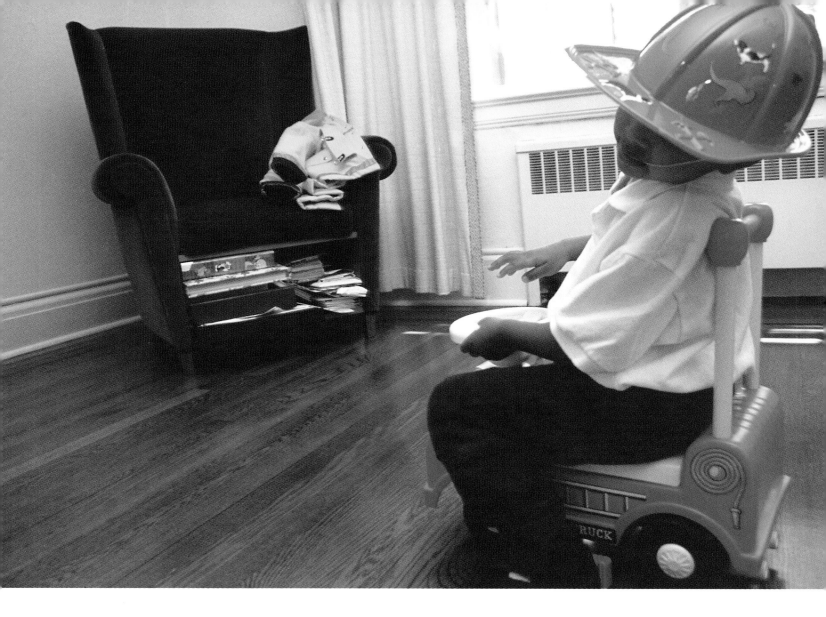

I ride my big, red fire truck.
**ZOOM ZOOM BARRUMMM!**
But I want to ride with Sarah.

# BANG-

## Whirr-
## Whirr-
## Crunch-Crunch.

**Who is that?**
**What is that?**
**Is it Sarah?**

No, it isn't Sarah.
It's the garbage truck
grinding up the garbage.
BANG-Whirr-Whirr-Crunch. Crunch.
When will Sarah come?

I don't want my crayons.
I don't want my book.
I don't want my blocks.
I don't want my bear.
I don't want
my big, red fire truck.

I want Sarah.

**I go outside
with Grandmom.
We watch.
We wait for Sarah.**

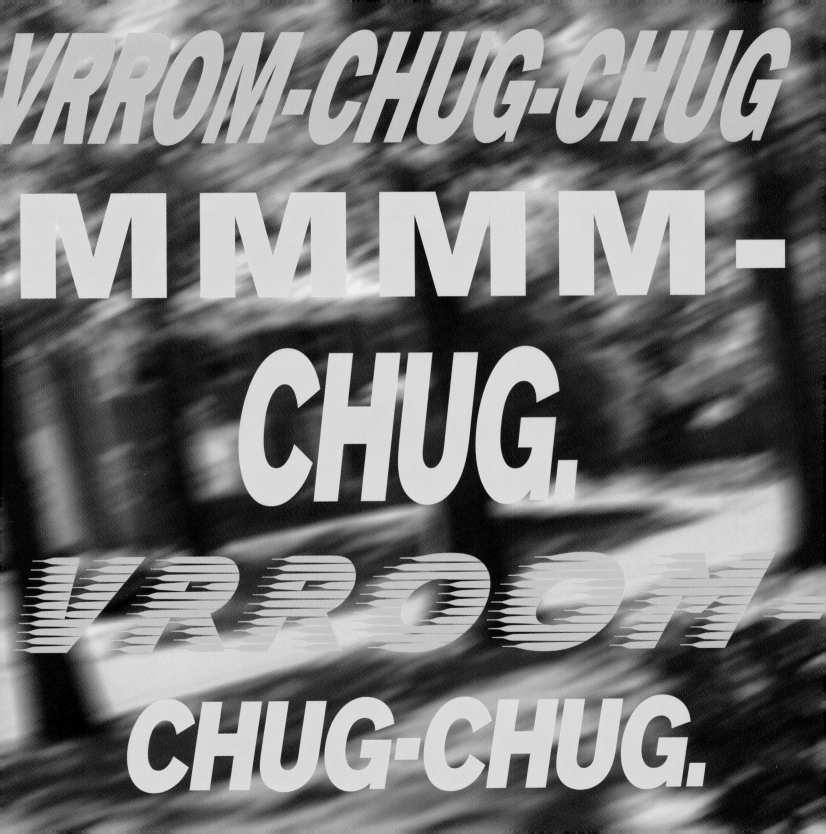

**A yellow school bus
is coming!
The bus is stopping.
The bus is stopping!**

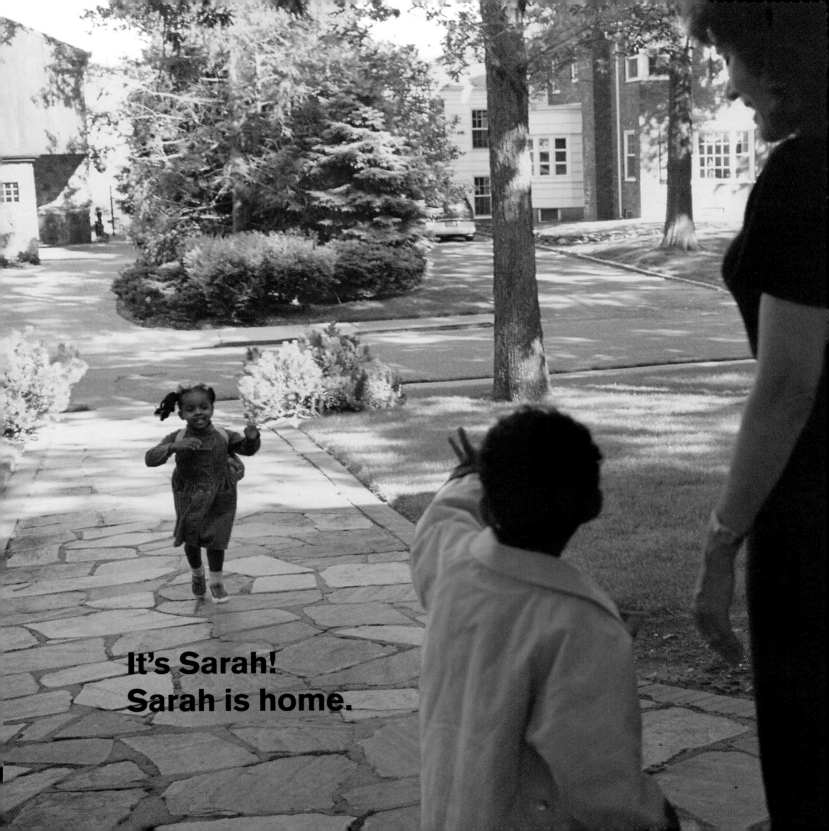

It's Sarah!
Sarah is home.

# ZOOM ZOOM BARRUMM!